XO, OX

A Love Story

Adam Rex

Pictures by
Scott Campbell

A NEAL PORTER BOOK
ROARING BROOK PRESS
NEW YORK

Text copyright © 2017 by Adam Rex
Illustrations copyright © 2017 by Scott Campbell
A Neal Porter Book
Published by Roaring Brook Press
Roaring Brook Press is a division of Holtzbrinck Publishing Holdings Limited Partnership
175 Fifth Avenue, New York, New York 10010
The art for this book was created using watercolor and colored pencil on paper.
mackids.com

Library of Congress Cataloging-in-Publication Data

Names: Rex, Adam. | Campbell, Scott, 1973– illustrator.
Title: XO, OX : a love story / [Adam Rex], Scott Campbell.
Description: First edition. | New York : Roaring Brook Press, 2017. | "A Neal
    Porter book." | Summary: "The hilarious tale of an ox who is in love with
    a gazelle, told in correspondence"— Provided by publisher.
Identifiers: LCCN 2016024228 | ISBN 9781626722880 (hardback)
Subjects: | CYAC: Love—Fiction. | Oxen—Fiction. | Gazelles—Fiction. |
    Letters—Fiction. | Humorous stories. | BISAC: JUVENILE FICTION / Humorous
    Stories. | JUVENILE FICTION / Love & Romance. | JUVENILE FICTION / Animals
    / Deer, Moose & Caribou.
Classification: LCC PZ7.R32865 Xo 2017 | DDC [E]—dc23
LC record available at https://lccn.loc.gov/2016024228

Our books may be purchased in bulk for promotional, educational, or business use. Please
contact your local bookseller or the Macmillan Corporate and Premium Sales Department
at (800) 221-7945 ext. 5442 or by e-mail at MacmillanSpecialMarkets@macmillan.com
First edition 2017
Printed in China by RR Donnelley Asia Printing Solutions Ltd., Dongguan City, Guangdong Province

3 5 7 9 10 8 6 4 2

For Marie, my love
—A.R.

For Eve. Thank you for your inspiring me
with your strength and imagination.
—S.C.

Dear Gazelle,

For some time now I have wanted to write a letter to say how much I admire you. You are so graceful and fine. Even when you are running from tigers you are like a ballerina who is running from tigers.

I think that what I am trying to say is that I love you.

XO,
OX

Dear <u>Ox</u>,

Thank you for your letter. I hope you understand that I have many admirers and cannot reply to each one personally.

Please enjoy the signed photo of me that I have enclosed for your collection.

Au revoir,
Gazelle

Dear Gazelle,

I DO understand that you must have many, <u>many</u> admirers and cannot reply to each letter personally. So it means SO much that you replied personally to mine.

XO,
OX

Dear <u>Ox</u>,

Thank you for your letter. I hope you understand that I have many admirers and cannot reply to each one personally.

Please enjoy the signed photo of me that I have enclosed for your collection.

Au revoir,
Gazelle

Dear Gazelle,

This is an amazing coincidence! I have written you two letters, and both times you have written back using the exact same words!

I think this shows that you are very smart and have a tidy mind. I hope that what I wrote before did not cause you to think that I only love you because you are pretty—I also love you because you are smart.

XO,
OX

Dear Ox,

Thank you again for your letter and your compliments.

Though I have many faults, I would not want anyone to think that I am repetitive. So here is a third and final letter, different from the first two.

There is no need to write me again.

Au revoir,
Gazelle

Dear Gazelle,

I will tell you, I almost fell out of my chair laughing when you said you have many faults. That is ridiculous. If you ask _me_, you have only one or two faults.

XO,
OX

Dear Ox,

You have made a mistake. I suppose you cannot help it, since you are an ox and probably have a clumsy brain.

But when I say that I have many faults, people usually like to tell me that I do not have any faults at all.

(Unlike some animals who may have many faults, such as that they are too large and too stout, and have strong smells about them, and clumsy brains.)

Au revoir,
Gazelle

Dear Gazelle,

I think I understand what you meant by your last letter, and I thank you for your honesty. I DO have many faults. I think it's important that I know what they are.

You make me want to be the best ox I can be. So I thank you again—you are the unflattering light of my life.

I eagerly await your next letter.

XO,
OX

Dear Ox,

There will be no next letter. I am not writing you anymore.

This letter doesn't count.

Au revoir,
Gazelle

Dear Gazelle,

Your sense of humor is a delight! Did I tell you already that I love your sense of humor? Plus your beauty and your mind.

XO,
OX

Ox! Stop this!

Please do not write me again. You are wasting your time.

I could never love a clumsy thing. I could never love a smelly thing. I could never love an animal that is too large, and too stout, and who is . . . so thick and ungraceful and awful and unlovely. And unlovable.

I could never, ever love an ox.

Dear Gazelle,

I know you couldn't.

But I think it is good that you've admitted one of your faults.
It makes me love you even more.

XO,
OX

Dear Ox,